ELLEN
AND THE
GOLDFISH

Story and Pictures by
John Himmelman

Harper & Row, Publishers

Ellen and the Goldfish
Copyright © 1990 by John Himmelman
Printed in the U.S.A. All rights reserved.
Typography by Patricia Tobin
10　9　8　7　6　5　4　3　2　1
First Edition

Library of Congress Cataloging-in-Publication Data
Himmelman, John.
　　Ellen and the goldfish : story and pictures / by John Himmelman.
　　　　p.　　cm.
　　Summary: A young girl, who loves to draw, befriends a goldfish
and uses her drawings to help him escape from the fishermen.
　　ISBN 0-06-022416-9 : $　　　. — ISBN 0-06-022417-7 (lib bdg.) : $
　　[1. Goldfish—Fiction.　2. Fishes—Fiction.　3. Drawing—Fiction.]
I. Title.
PZ7.H5686E1　1990　　　　　　　　　　　　　　　　　89-34475
[E]—dc20　　　　　　　　　　　　　　　　　　　　　　　　CIP
　　　　　　　　　　　　　　　　　　　　　　　　　　　　AC

To my "Little Bits,"

whose smiles will always brighten my world

Ellen loved to draw.
Her favorite place to draw was by a small pond
that was next to a big lake.

One morning, she noticed a goldfish watching her.

She waved to him, but the goldfish swam away.

The next morning, the goldfish came back.
Ellen drew a picture for him,
and the goldfish seemed to like it.

Then the goldfish disappeared again.
Ellen waited a long time, but he didn't come back.

The next time Ellen went to the pond,
she found the goldfish waiting for her.

She sat down slowly and drew a picture.
The goldfish stayed and watched her.

All day long she drew,
and all day long the goldfish watched her.

Ellen started to come to the pond every day.
The goldfish was always waiting for her.

She drew all kinds of things for him.

The goldfish loved her drawings.

Most of the time.

The two of them became very good friends.

Then one morning when Ellen got to the pond,
a couple of boys were fishing on the other side.

"Why don't you fish in the big lake?" she asked.
"Nobody does. There's too many weeds,"
said one of the boys.

Ellen was afraid that her friend might get caught.
She tried to warn him with pictures.

But the goldfish didn't seem to understand.

The next morning, Ellen came with a bag of crackers.
She wanted to make sure
he would be too full to eat the bait.

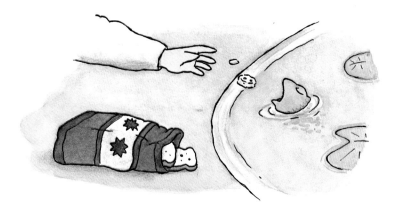

She fed him,

and fed him,

and fed him.

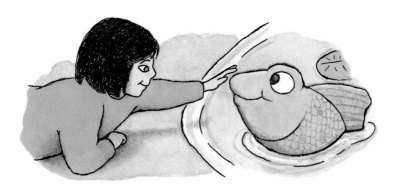

And the goldfish grew bigger and bigger and bigger.

One afternoon, the boys saw the giant goldfish.

The news spread fast.
Ellen knew it was just a matter of time
before her friend got caught.

She drew him one more picture.

She held it up over the water
and hoped the goldfish would see it.

Suddenly, there was a big splash!

The goldfish jumped out of the pond,
over their heads, and into the big lake.

Everyone cast their lines into the lake,
but the lines got tangled in the weeds.

As Ellen walked home along the lake,
she heard another splash. She waved to the goldfish.
"See you tomorrow," she said.

31